Mission Statement

You are the hero of this mission.

Each section of this book is numbered. At the end of most sections, you will have to make a choice. The choice you make will take you to a different section of the book.

Some of your choices will help you to complete your mission successfully. But if you make the wrong choice, death may be the best you can hope for! Because even that is better than being UNDEAD and becoming a slave of the monsters you have sworn to destroy!

Dare you go up against a world of monsters?

All right, then.

Let's see what you've got...

Introduction

You are an agent of **G.H.O.S.T.** — Global Headquarters Opposing Supernatural Threats.

Our world is under constant attack from supernatural horrors that lurk in the shadows. It's your job to make sure they stay there.

You have studied all kinds of monsters, and know their habits and behaviour. You are an expert in disguise, able to move among monsters in human form as a spy. You are expert in all forms of martial arts. G.H.O.S.T. has supplied you with weapons, equipment and other assets that make you capable of destroying any supernatural creature.

G.H.O.S.T.

HERO

MONSTER HUNTER
GHOST

STEVE BARLOW AND STEVE SKIDMORE
ILLUSTRATED BY PAUL DAVIDSON

Franklin Watts
First published in Great Britain in 2018
by The Watts Publishing Group

Text © Steve Barlow and Steve Skidmore 2018
Illustrations © The Watts Publishing Group 2018
Cover design: Cathryn Gilbert
Executive Editor: Adrian Cole

ISBN 978 1 4451 5939 3
ebook ISBN 978 1 4451 5940 9
Library ebook ISBN 978 1 4451 5941 6

1 3 5 7 9 10 8 6 4 2

Printed in Great Britain

Franklin Watts
An imprint of
Hachette Children's Group
Part of The Watts Publishing Group
Carmelite House
50 Victoria Embankment
London EC4Y 0DZ

An Hachette UK Company
www.hachette.co.uk

www.franklinwatts.co.uk

You are based at Arcane Hall, a spooky mansion. Your butler, Cranberry, is another G.H.O.S.T. agent who assists you in your adventures, providing you with information and backup.

Your life at Arcane Hall is comfortable and peaceful; but you know that at any moment, the G.H.O.S.T. High Command can order you into action in any part of the world...

Go to 1.

1

You are taking a well-earned day off from saving the world. You are on a private tour of the Tower of London, home to the Crown Jewels of the British monarchy.

Your guide is a Yeoman of the Guard. He is holding a pike and tells you of the Tower's gruesome history.

"Many people were executed at the Tower, including three queens!" he says. "And they were not happy about it!"

"How do you know?" you ask, jokingly. "Did they tell you?"

"As a matter of fact, yes they did." He stares at you strangely. "Do you believe in ghosts?"

You nod, thinking about all those ghosts you've had to deal with. In your time as an agent you've faced CGs (Cute Ghosts) NGs (Nasty Ghosts) and RNGs (**Really** Nasty Ghosts).

"Of course," you reply.

"I'm glad to hear it!" He emits a low growling noise and you realise that you can see through his body! He is a ghost but the pike he's holding is real and he's pointing it at you!

"Monster Hunter, we have been waiting for you!" he growls. "The hunter is the hunted!"

You are astounded. How did this thing know who you are? You know you need to act quickly, but you have left your weapons in your car.

If you wish to use your martial arts skills to fight the ghost, go to 15.

If you wish to head out of the Tower to get your weapons, go to 37.

You throw a GAG grenade towards the ghost and start to blast it with your BAM gun.

The night air is filled with the sound of explosions and shrieking laughter. The attack has no effect. The grenade and bullets are absorbed into the body of the Lady of the White Tower.

"You are too late, Hunter," she laughs.

You gasp in horror as the GAG grenade heads back towards you, followed by the bullets you fired. The deadly ammunition rips into your body. Thankfully, the pain is only temporary as the grenade explodes.

Ouch! Go back to 1.

3

"What is behind this ghostly infestation?" you ask.

The ghost snarls. "You will never know, Hunter. Our mistress will defeat you and find the orb. Then the walls of the Tower will no longer confine us. We will have our revenge on the living."

"That's the problem with you ghosts," you smile. "Always boasting. You just can't keep things to yourselves. A mistress, revenge and an orb. That's more than enough to be getting on with. Thank you and goodbye."

Go to 23.

4

You unclip a couple of GAGs and hurl them at the oncoming enemy. There is a huge explosion and the room is filled with flames. Too late, you realise that the armoury was too small to use these weapons in. There is another explosion and you, and the royal armoury, are obliterated.

You got rid of the ghosts, but you got rid of you as well! Go back to 1.

5

You hear screaming from the entrance to the Tower. Dozens of people pour out of the building as they are chased down by several ghostly creatures!

You aim your BAM (Blast All Monsters) gun, but realise you can't fire in case you hit any of the fleeing crowd. Taking advantage of your helplessness, the ghosts fly over the people's heads towards you! Before you can take aim, you are hit by a wave of ghostly forms. They spin you around and you hear a ghostly chant in your head: "Hunter, you are ours! You are ours!"

The voices grow louder and louder. They are the last thing you hear as you lose consciousness... and your life.

Why did you hang around? Go back to 1.

6

"So, you want me to come to you, then I will," you mutter to yourself, checking your weapons. "But be careful what you wish for!"

You head into the White Tower and climb the stairs to the royal armoury.

Hundreds of swords and axes line the walls. Dozens of suits of armour stand behind glass walls and sit astride models of armoured warhorses.

As you step in, the room begins to shake. You can hardly keep your balance as the weapons detach themselves from the walls and float in mid-air, pointing at you!

To get out of the room immediately, go to 38.

To use the APE (Anti-Poltergeist Equipment), go to 24.

7

"I am the Hunter! It is me that you seek! Put the child down," you shout at the ghost.

The ghost doesn't respond and you suddenly realise why — it has no head so can't hear or see you! The ghost turns and heads away from the crowd, with the terrified child in its grip.

To use your BAM gun, go to 11.

To chase after the ghost, go to 25.

8

You take aim and shoot at the smaller orb. It explodes into thousands of pieces, but has no effect on the Lady of the White Tower.

You chose the wrong orb! Before you can rectify your mistake, the Lady breaks free of the electrical chains. She lets out a demonic scream that reverberates through the Tower, causing you to drop to the ground.

The ghosts respond to her beckoning, flying into her one by one, to be absorbed by their mistress as she grows bigger and bigger!

You look up to see her monstrous foot above your body. She stamps down on you and you feel your soul being sucked into the ghostly mass as you too become part of the soul of the Tower.

It was a fifty-fifty call, but you got it wrong! **Go back to 1.**

9

Before you can move, the ghost hurls his pike at you.

You feel a great pain and then... nothing. You too have joined the ranks of those in the Tower who have lost their lives by a sharp weapon!

Go back to 1.

10

You decide not to respond further to the beckoning figure and start to move on. However, before you can get away, the the air is filled with screeching as the ghostly lady swoops down, heading towards you.

"Follow me!" she cries. The supernatural spook is immediately joined by dozens of other ghostly creatures pouring out the windows of the Tower.

You blast at the creatures with your BAM gun, but there are too many of them to deal with.

The creatures engulf you, knocking your weapon from your grip and choking you with their grasping hands.

Go to 48.

11

You raise your gun, but before you can shoot, a woman knocks it from your hand. "What are you doing? That's my son!"

You realise that she is right; by shooting at the moving target, you would risk hitting the child. You pick up your weapon.

"Apologies, ma'am, you're right!"

Go to 25.

12

You race down the stairs, head out of the White Tower and sprint towards the Jewel House. As you do so, you contact Cranberry for any intel he can provide.

"I'm afraid the identity of the Lady of the White Tower is still a mystery," he says.

"What about the orb?" you ask. "Is it part of the Crown Jewels?"

"Yes, but there is a problem. There are two orbs: the Sovereign's Orb and a smaller one, made for Queen Mary II. She could mean either of them."

"Hmmm, so it's a fifty-fifty choice. Stick around, I might have to phone a friend."

At that moment, the courtyard is filled with a kaleidoscope of colour. Stars and beams of energy whirl around as the Lady of the Tower emerges from the Jewel House. She is wearing the Imperial State Crown and holds the two orbs, one in each hand.

"You are too late, Hunter," she cries. "I have the orb! And now you will see what powers I have."

If you want to attack the ghost immediately, go to 2.

If you want to play for time, go to 34.

13

You head off towards the White Tower, but as you do so, you hear a loud trumpeting sound.

You spin around and gasp in astonishment. An ectoplasmic elephant is charging towards you! It is closely followed by a pack of banshee baboons and a phantom polar bear! You know that there was once a zoo in the Tower and quickly realise that these are the ghosts of the animals that once lived there.

The spooky creatures head towards you, teeth bared...

To use the GOSH (Ghosts and Other Spooks Handler), go to 35.

To use the GAG (Ghosts All Gone) grenade, go to 45.

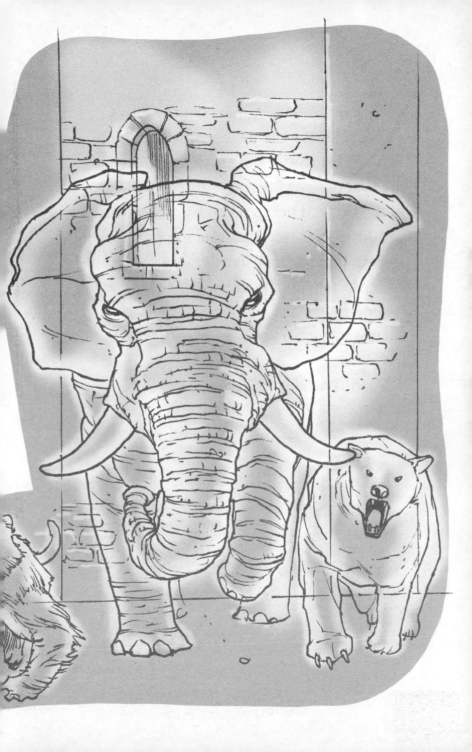

You throw the GAG at the alligator.

It catches it in its jaws and, with a shake of its head, tosses the weapon over the battlements. The GAG explodes harmlessly as the alligator leaps at you. It brings its ghostly jaws down on your torso! Instead of passing through your body, they rip through your flesh!

You scream in pain as the Lady of the White Tower laughs hysterically at your suffering. It is the last thing you hear as you pass into blackness and oblivion.

Ouch! That hurt. Go back to 1.

15

Avoiding the pike you leap at the ghostly guard, but pass straight through its body! You spin around to see the ghost floating above your head. It pulls back its arm and aims the pike at you!

To run to the car to get your weapons, go to 37.

To continue the fight, go to 9.

16

In the blink of an eye, you fire at the ghostly King of the Jungle, blasting it into ectoplasmic goo.

You look around the deserted grounds. The tourists seem to have fled from the castle grounds and you can see no signs of further paranormal activity in the vicinity.

You check in with Cranberry and tell him about the ghostly menagerie.

"They don't sound as though they belong to the Cute Ghost category, Agent," he says.

"Keep working on the intel," you tell him. "I want to know what other surprises might be heading my way."

"If you knew about them, then they wouldn't be surprises," replies Cranberry.

"Very funny, Cranberry," you say. "Keep working on the intel... and your jokes."
Go to 42.

17

You turn and run, but don't get very far as the ghosts swoop down on you, knocking your gun from your hand. You try to fight back, but it is hopeless. You are engulfed by the ghostly masses and are dragged to the Lady of the White Tower.
Go to 48.

18

You know there are too many ghosts to deal with without the proper weapons. You will have to play for time until the Spook Truck arrives.

You drop your BAM gun and hold up your hands.

"How do you know who I am?" you ask.

The ghostly Beefeater laughs.

"Your reputation goes before you in the world of the Undead," he replies. "There is a price on your head!"

You laugh and point at the headless ghost. "Well, he could certainly use one!"

At that moment, there is a crashing of wood as the Spook Truck smashes through the gates, sirens and lights flashing.

In the confusion, the ghosts take flight, leaving only the spooky Yeoman. He snarls and heads towards you, his weapon raised.

Reach for the BAM gun, go to 41.

Try to get to the weapons in the truck, go to 9.

19

The creature is almost upon you as you take out the GAG grenade and hurl it at the oncoming ghost. But as you throw it you realise that you've made a terrible mistake! You are too near the blast zone! There is a blinding flash of light and then silence as you too are blasted into oblivion.

That wasn't very clever! Go back to 1.

20

Instinct takes over and you dive out of the way, narrowly avoiding the deadly lance.

The horse comes screeching to a halt as the knight tries to turn the ghostly mount around.

Taking advantage, you clip in another magazine of AGGRO and blast away at your supernatural enemy, turning rider and horse into molten metal.

You check that there are no more ghostly surprises in the armoury and then head up the stairs to the battlements to hunt down the Lady of the White Tower.

Go to 29.

21

You race back into the Tower to be met by a crowd of terrified tourists running towards you. They are fleeing from a flying headless ghost that is trying to grab them with its spindly arms.

To shoot at the ghost with your BAM gun, go to 28.

To wait for the crowd to pass you, go to 44.

22

You take aim and shoot at the Sovereign's Orb.

It explodes into thousands of pieces and, as it does, the Lady of the White Tower lets forth a demonic scream that reverberates through the night sky.

She sparks with electricity and a whirlwind spins around her body, sucking it up and breaking it into pieces.

The ghosts of the Tower are drawn into this maelstrom as it sucks them up high above the Tower's grounds. There is a second's pause before the spinning cloud explodes and ectoplasm falls like torrential rain.

Then there is silence. You pick yourself up and wipe at the slimy goo.

"I hate that!" you mutter.

Go to 50.

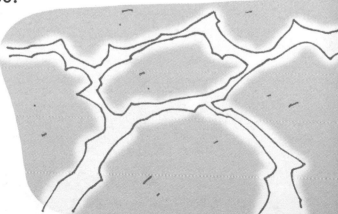

23

Snarling, the ghost attacks. You blast it with the BAM gun. A shower of ectoplasm rains down on you.

"I hate that bit," you groan, wiping the grisly remains from your clothes.

Cranberry's voice crackles in your ear. "I presume the truck has arrived. Is everything satisfactory, Agent?"

"Impeccable timing, Cranberry, as always," you reply.

"I try my best, Agent."

If you questioned the ghostly Yeoman, go to 39.

If you didn't, go to 49.

24

You quickly take out your Anti-Poltergeist Equipment and press the small black button. Blue and green laser beams and electromagnetic charges pulse and surge through the air, swirling and engulfing every sword, axe and spear in the room. The weapons clatter harmlessly to the floor and you switch off the APE.

But just when you think you are safe, there is a crashing sound as the air is filled with shards of glass. Instinctively, you shield your eyes. Seconds later you open them and gasp in horror — the suits of armour are heading towards you! At the same time, you hear a neighing sound. The model horses rear up, before their armoured knights turn them around to face you!

To use the GAG (Ghosts All Gone) grenade, go to 4.

To use the APE (Anti-Poltergeist Equipment) again, go to 43.

To use AGGRO (Aggressive Ghost and Ghoul Reduction Ordnance) in your BAM gun, go to 31.

25

You sprint after the ghost as it flies off into the heart of the Tower's grounds, following it through the entrance into the inner courtyard.

You screech to a halt. There are dozens of ghosts floating before you! The headless ghost drops the child, who runs off.

The Yeoman ghost steps out of the throng of

ghostly forms. "You fell into our trap, Hunter!
Surrender!"

At that moment you hear Cranberry's voice
via your comms link. "Spook Truck arrival in two
minutes."

To surrender to the ghosts, go to 18.

To fight them, go to 9.

In your hurry to stop the ghost reaching the Jewel Room, you leap from the battlements and realise immediately that you have made a big mistake!

You plunge downwards, hit the ground and pass out.

Some time later you wake up to find yourself floating above the ground. You have become a ghost!

Leaping off a building! What were you thinking? Go back to 1.

You decide to find the orbs and head towards the Jewel House.

The ghostly lady reappears on the roof of the White Tower and once again beckons you to her.

"Hunter, come to me."

Should you do as the lady says? She's almost certainly luring you into a trap.

Once more she beckons.

"Hunter, I grow impatient."

Go to 10.

28

You aim your BAM at the spook, but at that moment it swoops down and grasps hold of a child. The terrified kid screams as it is plucked into the air by the headless ghost.

To challenge the ghost to fight you, go to 7.

To use your BAM gun, go to 11.

29

The sun has now set as you step out into the cold night air to see the figure of the Lady of the White Tower. She holds a leash on the end of which is a huge alligator!

Another member of the ghostly menagerie, you think to yourself.

"Welcome, Hunter!" she smiles. "What a shame it will be such a brief meeting." She releases the leash. "Attack, my beauty!"

The alligator scuttles towards you, jaws open.

To use a GAG, go to 14.

To use the GOSH, go to 40.

30

Again you unleash bolts of energy, which engulf the ghostly elephant. It trumpets its defiance, but this time it cannot break free.

The other creatures still struggle against their bonds, but they are helpless against the GOSH machine's force.

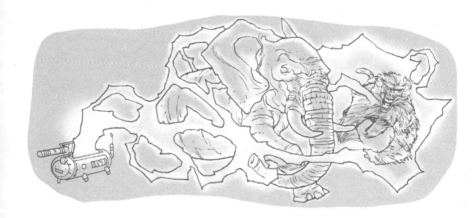

You take out your BAM gun and finish off the ghostly menagerie. At that moment though, you hear a roar, as from out of the shadows a huge ghostly lion bounds towards you.

To use the GAG grenade, go to 19.

To use the BAM gun, go to 16.

31

You clip a magazine of AGGRO into your BAM gun and begin firing at the ghostly armour.

Within seconds the floor is littered with lumps of twisted metal as the AGGRO lives up to its name.

A scrapyard would pay a fortune for this lot, you think. But at that moment you hear the thundering of hooves and you spin around to see a knight on an armoured horse charging towards you. He holds out a deadly lance, which is pointing at you!

You smile, aim your BAM gun and pull the trigger, but nothing happens — you've run out of AGGRO!

To clip on another magazine of AGGRO, go to 36.

To dive out of the way, go to 20.

"The Lady of the White Tower," you mutter to yourself.

As the creature continues to taunt you, Cranberry's voice crackles in your ear.

"Agent, I think the orb that the ghostly Yeoman mentioned is part of the Crown Jewels. And I've not found anything more on this Lady of the White Tower."

"Don't worry, Cranberry," you reply. "She's found me."

To head into the White Tower, go to 6.

To head towards the Crown Jewels House, go to 27.

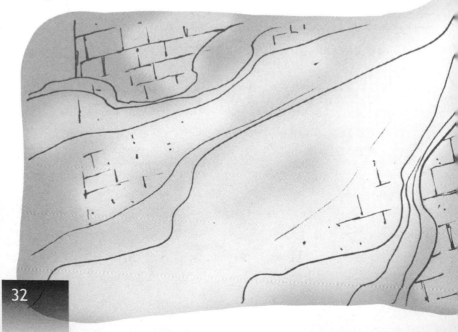

33

You decide that you need as many weapons as possible. "Come on Cranberry, where's the truck?"

"It's on hyper auto-drive but the London traffic is heavy. It's going to be some time before it gets to you."

If you want to continue to wait for the truck, go to 5.

To grab what weapons you have and head back into the Tower, go to 47.

34

"Who are you?" you ask. "And what do you want?"

"I am the soul of the Tower," the Lady replies. "I am the consciousness of everyone and everything that has perished within these walls. I have absorbed their sorrow for centuries, growing in strength, growing in power."

"What about the orb?" you ask. "Why do you need that?"

"The orb is the vessel to rule and bring together the dead of the Tower."

"So why wait until this moment?" you ask.

"I needed one final soul to give me the power to control the Undead — you! The knowledge you have of the supernatural will transfer to me and so I will have ultimate power!"

"I'm flattered," you reply as, out of the ghost's view, you slowly clip an AGGRO magazine into the BAM gun.

"And now you are here and you are too late to stop me!" she laughs.

"Better late than never," you say.

"Not this time, Hunter! Come to me, my

children!" she cries. The sky is instantly filled with hundreds of ghosts, swirling and swooping in answer to their mistress's summons.

To attack the Lady of the White Tower, go to 2.

To get out of there now, go to 17.

To use the GOSH on the Lady of the White Tower, go to 46.

35

You take out the GOSH, point it at the oncoming supernatural creatures and squeeze the trigger. Bolts of energy shoot out of the machine, wrapping around the creatures, and restraining them in chains of fluorescent plasma.

However, there are too many ghosts for just one blast of the machine and they are too powerful. The elephant breaks free of the energy chains and charges at you.

To use the GAG, go to 19.

To use the GOSH again, go to 30.

36

You reach into your pack and pull out another magazine of AGGRO. But you are too slow. The ghostly warrior is upon you! You give a cry as the deadly lance pierces your body and pins you to the floor.

Wracked with pain, you can only stare in horror as the knight dismounts, picks up an axe and heads towards you. With one swing of the weapon, your agony is relieved.

That hurt! Go back to 1.

You dodge the pike and sprint out of the Tower. The ghost howls in frustration.

As you run towards the exit, you contact Cranberry on the mobile comms link.

"You sound a little stressed," he says. "Is there anything troubling you?"

You tell him about the ghost. "It was a Yeoman of the Guard — you know, a Beefeater..."

"Strictly speaking," says Cranberry, "the Beefeaters are the Yeoman Warders. The Yeomen of the Guard are a different..."

"I don't care! Get the Spook Truck here ASAP and get some intel on the ghosts that might be hanging around this place. I need to understand how they know about me."

You reach your car and open the boot. You have one or two weapons that may help you fight the ghost, but the main anti-ghost arsenal is in the Spook Truck.

To wait for the Spook Truck to arrive, go to 33.

To head back into the Tower, go to 47.

38

You turn, but you are too slow. Hundreds of axes, spears and swords fly towards you. Their sharp metal tips tear into your body, leaving you well and truly skewered.

You shouldn't have run — the point has been made! Go back to 1.

39

You tell Cranberry what the ghostly Yeoman revealed before you blasted it.

"Hmm, looks like we have a case of a RNG. I've run a full Spook Scan on the Tower and it seems it's full of ghostly activity. There are hundreds of paranormal readings on our scanners! There's also a mention in the historical records of a ghostly Lady in the White Tower."

"She might be the mistress the Yeoman mentioned," you say. "Try and find out what the orb could be and I'll look for the head spook."

You open the Spook Truck and load up with the weapons that you'll need to fight these ghostly enemies.

Go to 13.

40

You point the GOSH at the advancing alligator and switch it on. Chains of energy shoot out and restrain the ghostly creature.

   You manoeuvre it up and over the battlements, where it hangs in the air. You take out a GAG, throw it into the creature's open jaws and switch off the GOSH. The alligator plummets towards the ground before exploding in a ball of flame.

The Lady of the White Tower screams at you. "You may have defeated my creature, but once I have the orb, you will be powerless against me!" She leaps off the battlements, heading towards the Jewel House.

To jump from the battlements after her, go to 26.

To head down the stairs, go to 12.

41

In one movement you reach down, pick up your BAM gun and point it at the ghost.

It stops and raises the pike.

"One move and I'll turn you into a spook smoothie," you warn.

To question the ghost, go to 3.

To blast it with the BAM gun, go to 23.

42

You decide to head towards the White Tower, at the centre of the castle grounds. As you do so, you look up and see the ghostly figure of a lady on the roof, passing along the battlements. She beckons to you.

You immediately drop to your knees and aim your BAM gun but the figure disappears before you can take a shot at it.

The figure reappears, at a window this time, and once again beckons you. Her voice rings out across the castle grounds. "Hunter, come to me!"

If you previously questioned the ghostly Yeoman, go to 32.

If you didn't, go to 10.

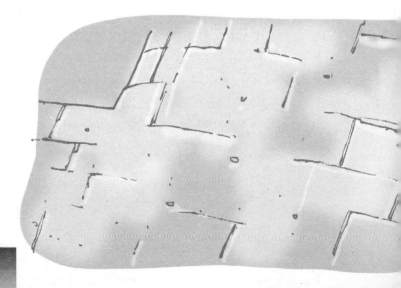

43

As the suits of armour stomp towards you, you press the small black button again on the APE.

Once more the room is filled with laser beams and electromagnetic charges. However, the armoured knights and horses are unaffected by this. You realise that these are not poltergeists the armour retains the imprint and memories of their former owners — these are ghosts!

To use the GAG (Ghosts All Gone) grenade, go to 4.

To use AGGRO (Aggressive Ghost and Ghoul Reduction Ordnance) in your BAM gun, go to 31.

You step into a recess in the castle wall and let the crowd rush by you. The ghost follows the crowd as you emerge from your hiding place and take aim with your BAM gun.

You squeeze the trigger and send an energy bolt at the monster. It explodes, covering the crowd with gloppy ectoplasm. They stop running but continue to scream!

"What did you do that for?" asks one of the tourists. "I'm covered in yucky ghost stuff!"

You roll your eyes. Some people are never satisfied. "You're welcome..." you say.

But as you do so another headless ghost swoops down.

Where do these keep coming from? you wonder.

The spook grasps hold of one of the young tourists. The terrified child screams as it is plucked into the air.

To challenge the ghost to fight you, go to 7.
To use your BAM gun, go to 11.

You take out a GAG grenade and hurl it at the supernatural creatures. There is a blinding flash and a loud "whump" that echoes around the ancient buildings. You open your eyes to see that the weapon has lived up to its name — the animal ghosts have all gone!

You smile to yourself and take out your BAM gun just in case there are more ghostly creatures to deal with. You are right to be cautious, as from out of the shadows a huge ghostly lion suddenly leaps at you!

To use the GAG grenade, go to 19.

To use the BAM gun, go to 16.

46

You drop your BAM gun and quickly pull out the GOSH device, point it at the Lady and switch it on. The ghost screams in fury as she is chained in swathes of light and energy.

"Do you think your puny chains can imprison me for very long?" she screams.

No, but I just needed some way to keep you still for a second, you think.

The ghosts scream and swirl through the night air as you pick up the BAM gun from the floor. "No time to phone a friend," you mutter, "it's trick or treat..."

To shoot at the Sovereign's Orb, go to 22.

To shoot at the smaller orb, go to 8.

47

Knowing that you can't afford to waste time, you grab hold of your BAM (Blast All Monsters) gun and head back towards the Tower's entrance.

To head to the place where you saw the ghostly Yeoman, go to 21.

To check out the Tower for more ghosts, go to 5.

48

The ghostly lady floats before you and grabs hold of your head with her hands. You are paralysed by her touch.

"Hunter, you have failed and now you will become one with me," she growls.

She opens her mouth and a stream of icy breath pours out, covering your head and filling your lungs. You feel your body go numb and your mind slipping away as you become yet another ghostly creature of the Tower.

She took your breath away! Go back to 1.

49

You tell Cranberry about the ghostly Yeoman.

"Hmm, looks like we have a case of an RNG. I've run a full Spook Scan on the Tower and it seems it's full of ghostly activity. There are hundreds of paranormal readings on our scanners!"

"I wonder what's causing that? Search the intel on the tower and get back to me when you find out anything that might help us. In the meantime, I'm going ghost hunting!"

You open the Spook Truck and load up with the weapons that you'll need to fight these ghostly enemies.

Go to 13.

50

You call Cranberry and tell him what happened.

"Why did you choose to shoot at the Sovereign's Orb?" he asks.

"I remember the ghost said something about the orb being the sovereign vessel to rule, so I guessed it had to be that one."

"That was a lucky choice..."

"Skill, Cranberry, sheer skill!"

"Are you going to continue with your holiday, Agent?" asks Cranberry.

You laugh. "No. I want to get back to work — being on holiday is too dangerous. Even for a G.H.O.S.T. agent!"

EQUIPMENT

Phantom Flyer: For fast international and intercontinental travel, you use the Phantom Flyer, a supersonic business jet crammed full of detection and communication equipment and weaponry.

Spook Truck: For more local travel you use one of G.H.O.S.T.'s fleet of Spook Trucks — heavily armed and armoured SUVs you requisition from local agents.

BAM — Blast All Monsters

GAG — Ghosts All Gone

AGGRO — Aggressive Ghost
and Ghoul Reduction
Ordnance

GOSH — Ghost and Other
Spooks Handler

APE — Anti-Poltergeist
Equipment

MONSTER HUNTER

I HERO

EDGE

VAMPIRE

STEVE BARLOW ◇ STEVE SKIDMORE
Illustrated by PAUL DAVIDSON

You are an agent of **G.H.O.S.T.** — Global Headquarters Opposing Supernatural Threats.

You know that back at Arcane Hall, Cranberry is searching all G.H.O.S.T.'s data for information.

"Remind me what we have on vampires," you say. "They're tough opponents, right?"

"You bet!" says Cranberry cheerfully. "Very fast and agile: but they can be destroyed by fire, holy water or a stake through the heart. Garlic slows them down. Only the light of dawn kills them instantly."

You check your flight plan. "I'm starting my final approach to Zurich."

"I'll have a fully-equipped Spook Truck waiting for you. Good luck!"

Continue the adventure in:

About the 2Steves

"The 2Steves" are
Britain's most popular
writing double act
for young people,
specialising in comedy
and adventure. They
perform regularly in schools and libraries,
and at festivals, taking the power of words
and story to audiences of all ages.

Together they have written many books,
including the *I HERO Immortals* and *iHorror* series.

About the illustrator:
Paul Davidson

Paul Davidson is a British
illustrator and comic book artist.

I HERO Legends — collect them all!

ATHENA

978 1 4451 5234 9 pb
978 1 4451 5235 6 ebook

BEOWULF

978 1 4451 5225 7 pb
978 1 4451 5226 4 ebook

KING ARTHUR

978 1 4451 5231 8 pb
978 1 4451 5232 5 ebook

FREYA

978 1 4451 5237 0 pb
978 1 4451 5238 7 ebook

HERCULES

978 1 4451 5228 8 pb
978 1 4451 5229 5 ebook

ROBIN HOOD

978 1 4451 5183 0 pb
978 1 4451 5184 7 ebook

Have you read the I HERO Toons series?

INVASION OF THE BOTTY SNATCHERS

978 1 4451 5927 0 pb
978 1 4451 5928 7 ebook

ENTER THE PENGUIN

978 1 4451 5924 9 pb
978 1 4451 5925 6 ebook

KILLER CUSTARD

978 1 4451 5930 0 pb
978 1 4451 5931 7 ebook

KUNG FU KITTEN

978 1 4451 5918 8 pb
978 1 4451 5919 5 ebook

ROBIN HAMSTER

978 1 4451 5921 8 pb
978 1 4451 5922 5 ebook

ATTACK of the ZOMBIE BUNNIES

978 1 4451 5873 0 pb
978 1 4451 5874 7 ebook

Also by the 2Steves...

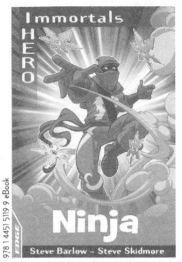

978 1 4451 5104 5 pb
978 1 4451 5119 9 eBook

You are a skilled, stealthy ninja. Your village has been attacked by a warlord called Raiden. Now YOU must go to his castle and stop him before he destroys more lives.

978 1 4451 5101 4 pb
978 1 4451 5117 5 eBook

You are the Warrior Princess. Someone wants to steal the magical ice diamonds from the Crystal Caverns. YOU must discover who it is and save your kingdom.

978 1 4451 5103 8 pb
978 1 4451 5121 2 eBook

You are a magical unicorn. Empress Yin Yang has stolen Carmine, the red unicorn. Yin Yang wants to destroy the colourful Rainbow Land. YOU must stop her!

978 1 4451 5102 1 pb
978 1 4451 5124 3 eBook

You are a spy, codenamed Scorpio. Someone has taken control of secret satellite laser weapons. YOU must find out who is responsible and stop their dastardly plans.